The author and publisher would like to thank Sue Ellis at the
Centre for Literacy in Primary Education for her input
and guidance during the making of this book.

First published 2011 by Walker Books Ltd
87 Vauxhall Walk, London SE11 5HJ

2 4 6 8 10 9 7 5 3 1

© 2011 Lucy Cousins
Lucy Cousins font © 2011 Lucy Cousins
The moral rights of the author/illustrator have been asserted.

Maisy™. Maisy is a registered trademark of Walker Books Ltd, London.

Printed in China

British Library Cataloguing in Publication Data:
a catalogue record for this book is available from the British Library

ISBN 978-1-4063-2727-4

www.walker.co.uk

Learn with Maisy

Lucy Cousins

WALKER BOOKS
AND SUBSIDIARIES
LONDON · BOSTON · SYDNEY · AUCKLAND

Maisy is having fun with

colours,
numbers,
shapes,
letters...
and chicks!

Would you like to join in?

4 5 6 7
8 9 10

How many chicks are there?

Spots and stripes

Zebra
is
stripy.

Who is spotty?

cloudy

sunny

snowy

stormy

windy

What kind of weather do you like?

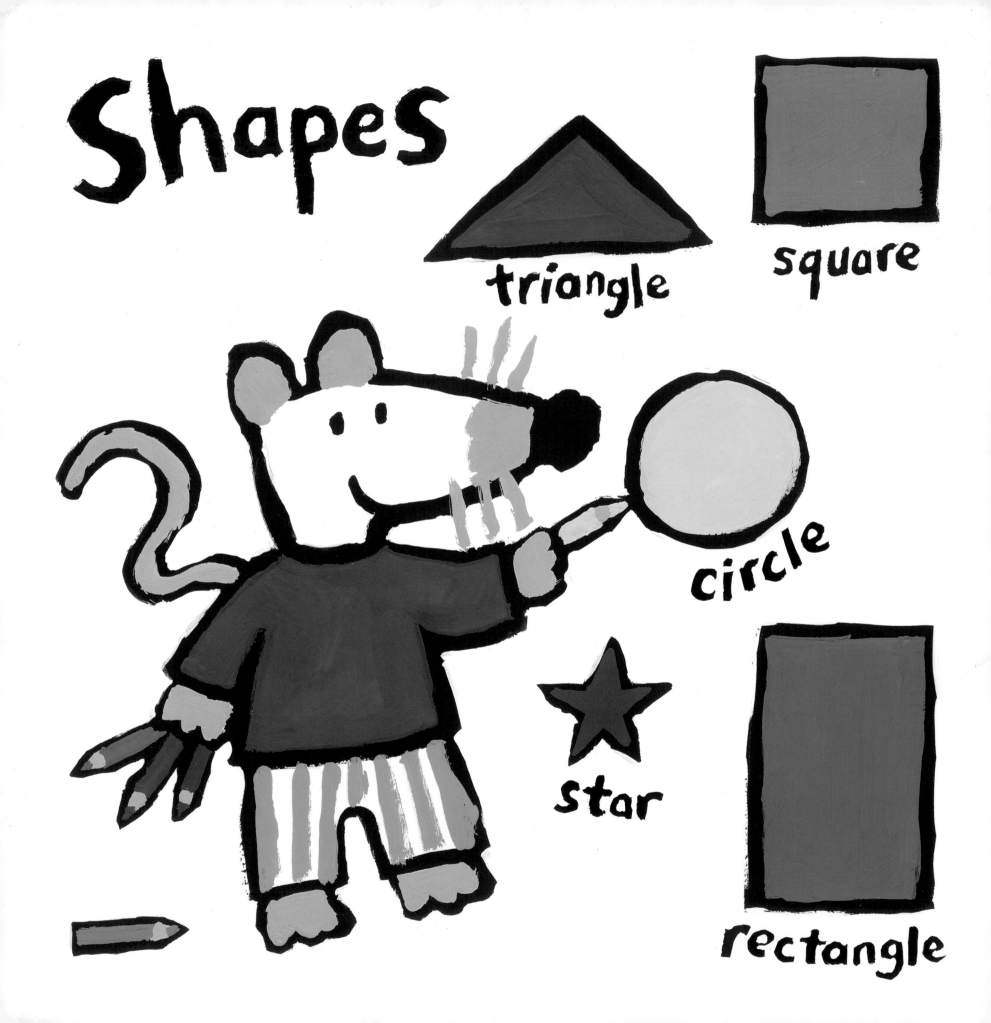

What shapes can you see?

Touch

Lamb feels soft and fluffy.

What do these feel like?

Counting

Maisy has two legs.

How many legs can you count?

Fast and slow

Tortoise is slow.

Days of the week

On Monday
Maisy plays football.

Animal noises

Bee says buzzzzzzz.

What do these animals say?

Colours

cheep

Chick is yellow.

Who is blue?
who is green?
who is brown?
Who is orange?
who is red?

Homes

Spider lives in a web.

Who lives in these homes?

shell

nest

underground

hive

Letters

Maisy begins with M.

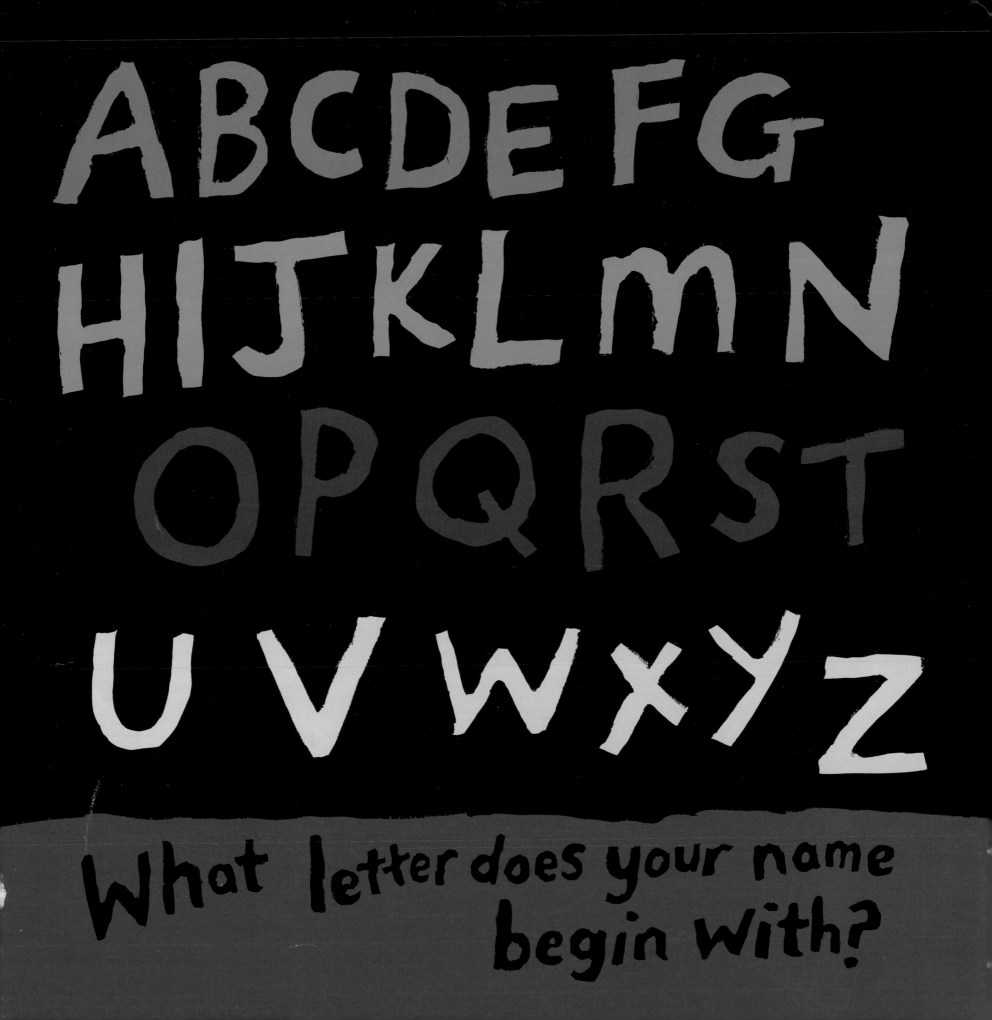

ABCDE FG
HIJKLMN
OPQRST
UVWXYZ

What letter does your name
begin with?

Can you make these quiet noises?

drip drip

tick-tock

purr purr

flitter-flutter

Who has sharp teeth?
Who has horns?
Who has a big tail?
Who has a shell?
Who has a long tongue?

cheep

Patterns

Maisy is hanging out the washing.

Can you match up the socks?

What have you learnt?

baa

one

slow

cold

moo

sunny

star

2 two

slimy

who is yellow?
Who is small?
Who says cheep?